Disney · PIXAR

TOY STORY

PaRragon

Bath · New York · Singapore · Hong Kong · Cologne · Delhi · Melbourne

This book belongs to

_____

Characters (in order of appearance)
Narrator   Tracey Fraim
Woody   Tom Hanks
Hamm   John Ratzenberg
Army Sergeant R. Lee Ermey
Buzz   Tim Allen
Rex   Wallace Shawn
Bo Peep   Annie Potts
Mr. Potato Head®   Don Rickles
Andy Davis   John Morris
Andy's Mum   Laurie Metcalf
Alien   Matthew Collins
Hannah   Sarah Freeman

Read-along Story Produced by Randy Thornton
Co-produced and Engineered by Jeff Sheridan
Adapted by Ron Kidd
℗ Walt Disney Records/Pixar
© Disney/Pixar. All rights reserved.

This edition published by Parragon in 2010
Parragon
Chartist House
15-17 Trim Street
Bath BA1 1HA, UK
www.parragon.com

ISBN 978-1-4454-0693-0

Printed in China

DISNEY · PIXAR

TOY STORY

Bath · New York · Singapore · Hong Kong · Cologne · Delhi · Melbourne

Every kid loves toys. Take Andy, for instance. He's got Rex the dinosaur, Hamm the piggy bank, Mr Potato Head, Slinky Dog and dozens of others. But his favourite toy is Woody, a cowboy doll who talks when Andy pulls his string. "Reach for the sky! This town ain't big enough for the two of us."

You probably like your toys, too. But did you ever wonder what they do when you leave the room? At Andy's house, the toys come alive!

One day, just before Andy's family was planning to move, Woody called the toys to order. "Okay, first item today. Has everyone picked a moving buddy? I don't want any toys left behind. A moving buddy – if you don't have one, get one! Oh, yes, one minor note here. Andy's birthday party's been moved to today."

The toys gasped. The change of plans meant that today Andy would be getting new toys. And if Andy got new toys, he might throw his old ones away. Woody, sensing panic, tried to calm everyone down. "I'm not worried. You shouldn't be worried."

Then Hamm waddled up. "Birthday guests at three o'clock!"

At Woody's command, a group of toy soldiers hustled downstairs, carrying a baby monitor. Upstairs, the toys heard a soldier's voice through the speaker, describing Andy's presents. "The bow's coming off. We've got a lunchbox here. Okay, second present…it appears to be…okay, it's bed sheets."

The toys seemed safe for another year. But there was one more surprise gift. "It's a huge package. Oh, wha – it's …it's a – "

Rex bumped the speaker and the batteries fell out. At the same time, there was a cheer from downstairs. The kids came racing upstairs to Andy's room as the toys scrambled back to their places.

Andy and his friends shoved Woody from his place on the bed and put a new toy there. They played with it, then raced back downstairs when it was time for games and prizes.

As the toys stirred, they heard a voice. "Buzz Lightyear to Star Command. Come in, Star Command. Why don't they answer?"

Woody climbed back up onto the bed and faced his worst fear: the coolest toy a kid could want, Buzz Lightyear. He gulped. "There has been a bit of a mix up. This is my spot, see, the bed here."

The other toys crowded around Buzz. Rex shook his hand. "Oh, I'm so glad you're not a dinosaur... Say! What's that button do?"

Buzz pressed the button and wings popped out. All the toys were impressed – except for Woody. "These are plastic. He can't fly!"

"Yes, I can. Stand back, everyone. To infinity and beyond!" Buzz leaped off the bed and headed straight for the floor. Then he bounced off a rubber ball and landed on a race car. The car took off on a track, spun through a loop and off a jump. Buzz flew out of the car, grabbing onto an aeroplane hung from the ceiling. After spinning around, he landed back on the bed. The toys cheered.

Woody couldn't believe it. "Well, in a couple of days, everything will be just the way it was. They'll see, I'm still Andy's favourite toy."

Suddenly, the sound of barking
interrupted the toys. They rushed
to the window. It was Scud, the
dog next door. With him was Sid, his
owner, a kid who loved
to torture toys.

Rex shook his head. "Oh, no. I can't bear to watch one of these again."

As the toys looked on helplessly, Sid strapped a firecracker to his Combat Carl toy, lit the fuse and blew the toy to smithereens. Sid cheered. "Yes! He's gone! He's history. That was very sweet. Did you see that, Scud?"

Bo Peep turned away. "The sooner we move, the better."

Late that afternoon, the family finished packing boxes. Andy's mum told him they were going to Pizza Planet, his favourite restaurant, for the last time. She said he could bring one toy. Woody, who was listening, knew it would be either him or Buzz.

Seeing a space between the edge of the desk and the wall, Woody got an idea. "Buzz … Buzz Lightyear, we've got trouble! A helpless toy – it's, it's trapped, Buzz!"

As Buzz leaned over the edge, Woody steered a remote control car towards him. Buzz dove out of the way, but the desk lamp swung around and accidentally knocked him out the window!

Mr Potato Head saw it all. "Couldn't handle Buzz cutting in on your playtime, could you, Woody? Didn't want to face the fact that Buzz just might be Andy's new favourite toy, so you got rid of him."

"No! Wait! I can explain everything."

Woody never had the chance because just then Andy came into the room. "Mum, do you know where Buzz is?"

"Just grab some other toy. Now, come on."

"Okay." Andy picked up Woody and carried him out to the van, past the bush where Buzz had landed. Buzz, seeing Andy take Woody into the van, raced after it and hopped on the back bumper.

The van pulled into a gas station and Andy got out, leaving Woody on the backseat. Woody looked up and saw Buzz, covered with mud, staring at him through the sunroof. "I just want you to know that even though you tried to terminate me, revenge is not an idea we promote on my planet."

Woody sighed with relief. "Oh. Oh, that's good."

"But we're not on my planet, are we?" Buzz lunged for Woody. The two of them fell off the seat, out the open door and rolled under the van. They were still on the ground, fighting, when the door slid shut and the van drove away.

Woody watched the van leave. "I'm lost! Oh, I'm a lost toy."

Buzz was upset for a different reason. "And you, my friend, are responsible for delaying my rendezvous with Star Command."

"You are a toy! You aren't the real Buzz Lightyear; you're ... you're an action figure. You are a child's plaything!"

Buzz shook his head. "You are a sad, strange little man and you have my pity. Farewell."

As Buzz walked off, a Pizza Planet delivery truck with a plastic rocket on its roof pulled into the station. Woody had found a way back to Andy, but Buzz had to go too. "Buzz! I found a spaceship!"

Buzz peered inside the truck. "Now, you're sure this space freighter will return to its port of origin once it jettisons its food supply?"

Woody nodded. "Uh-huh. And when we get there, we'll be able to find a way to transport you home."

Sure enough, the truck took them to its port of origin – Pizza Planet. Buzz looked around in amazement. "What a spaceport!"

Then Woody spotted Andy with his mum and baby sister, Molly. Seeing a basket on Molly's stroller, Woody grinned. "Okay, when I say go, we're going to jump in the basket." But Buzz was gone.

Buzz had spotted a game shaped like a rocket and thought it might take him home. Inside, he found himself surrounded by squeeze-toy aliens. "I am Buzz Lightyear. Who's in charge here?"

The aliens pointed up at a giant crane. "The claw is our master. The claw chooses who will go and who will stay. Shhhh! It moves."

Woody, who had followed Buzz into the game, gazed up in horror. "Oh, no! Sid!" Andy's cruel neighbour was at the controls.

The claw came down. It grabbed Buzz and pulled him upward. Woody clung to his legs, desperately trying to pull him free.

Sid was thrilled. "All right! Double prizes!"

Sid raced home with Woody and Buzz in his backpack. He tossed the pack onto his bed, shut the door and went downstairs.

Woody got out of the pack, ran across the bed and leaped onto the doorknob. "Locked! There's got to be another way out of here."

There was a noise behind him and a doll's head looked out from under the bed. Woody smiled. "Hi, there, little fella. Come out here. Do you know a way out of here?"

The head continued towards him, propelled by a creepy, spider-like body made from the pieces of an Erector set. In horror, Woody scrambled back up onto the bed. "B-B-B-Buzz!"

The doll was joined by other mutant toys assembled from parts that Sid had thrown to the floor. Woody jumped inside the backpack and Buzz zipped it shut, punching a button on his chest. "Mayday! Mayday! Come in, Star Command! Send reinforcements!" He adjusted his laser light and turned to Woody. "I've set my laser from stun to kill."

"Yeah, and if anyone attacks us we can blink 'em to death."

But instead of attacking, the mutant toys crept back out of sight. Woody and Buzz were safe … for the time being, at least.

The next morning, when Sid went downstairs, Woody jumped to his feet. "The door – it's open! We're free!"

He and Buzz raced for the hallway, but their path was blocked by the mutant toys. As the monsters approached, Buzz turned to Woody. "Shield your eyes!" He fired his laser. Nothing happened.

Woody shook his head in disgust. "Oh, you idiot – you're a toy! Use your karate chop action." Woody pushed a button on Buzz's back and Buzz's arms began chopping. The mutant toys backed away, giving Woody and Buzz room to slip through the door.

While Woody was scouting the hallway, Buzz ducked inside another room. Behind him, a voice rang out. "Calling Buzz Lightyear. This is Star Command." The voice was coming from a commercial on TV advertising Buzz Lightyear toys.

Woody had been right after all. Buzz was just a toy.

Stunned, Buzz staggered to the top of the stairs. He opened his wings and jumped, hoping to fly. Instead, he crashed to the floor.

By the time Woody found him, Buzz had been discovered by Sid's sister, Hannah. She had dressed him up for a tea party and given him a new name. "Would you like some tea, Mrs Nesbit?"

When Hannah left the room, Woody ran inside. He found Buzz with one arm. "Look at me. I can't even fly out of a window."

Woody smiled. "Out the window … Buzz, you're a genius!"

He dragged Buzz back into Sid's room, then stood in the window and called to Andy's house. "Hey, guys! Guys! Hey!"

When the toys appeared, Buzz wouldn't help. So Woody picked up Buzz's arm and waved it, as if Buzz were standing behind the window frame. "Hiya, fellas. To infinity and beyond!"

But Woody held the arm too high and Mr Potato Head saw that it had been broken off. "Murderer! You murdering dog!"

Once again, the toys believed that Woody had done something awful to Buzz. As they hurried away from the window, Woody tried to stop them. "You've got to help us, please! You don't know what it's like over here!" But it was no use. Before Woody could turn around, the mutants were all over Buzz.

Woody tried to stop them. "All right, back! Back, you cannibals!" But the toys grabbed Buzz's arm and pushed Woody aside.

When they backed away, Buzz's arm was in place! Woody couldn't believe it. "Hey! Hey, they fixed you!" He tried to thank the mutant toys, but they scrambled back under the bed.

Sid came into the room with a brand-new rocket. "What am I going to blow? Man … hey, where's that wimpy cowboy doll?"

As Woody hid under a milk crate, Sid spotted Buzz. He set his toolbox on the crate, trapping Woody. Then he picked up Buzz and taped the rocket to his back. "Yes! To infinity and beyond!"

There was a clap of thunder and it started to rain. Sid looked outside. "Aw, man." He sat at the window, waiting for it to stop.

Sid wasn't the only one hoping for sunshine. Next door, Andy and his mum had finished packing for their move the next day. Andy went to bed, sad that he never found his favourite toys.

While Andy and Sid slept, Woody called to Buzz for help. He lay with the rocket on his back, too sad to move. "I'm just a toy."

Woody glared at him. "Look, over in that house is a kid who thinks you are the greatest and it's not because you're a space ranger, pal. It's because you're a toy. You are his toy!"

A few moments later, the crate began to shake. Buzz was trying to push the toolbox off! "Come on, sheriff. There's a kid over in that house who needs us. Now, let's get you out of this thing!"

Just as Buzz managed to free Woody, Sid's alarm clock rang. Sid jumped out of bed, grabbed Buzz and headed outside.

As Sid's toys crept out from under the bed, Woody asked them for help. "Please, he's my friend, he's the only one I've got." The toys gathered around. "Okay, I think I know what to do and if it works, it'll help everybody."

Working together, they escaped to the backyard, where Sid was starting to light the rocket. Suddenly he saw Woody lying nearby. "Hey! How'd you get out here?"

As Sid watched, an army of mutant toys rose from the grass and marched towards him. Woody grinned. "From now on, you must take good care of your toys. Because if you don't, we'll find out, Sid."

Sid ran screaming into the house.

As Woody rushed to help Buzz, a car horn honked. Next door, Andy's family and their moving truck were leaving. Buzz, with the rocket still strapped to his back, motioned to Woody. "Come on!"

They raced after the truck and grabbed onto the back. Woody held on, but Buzz fell to the street. "Buzz!" Thinking fast, Woody found Andy's toy box inside and dug out the remote-controlled car. He tossed it into the street and steered it towards Buzz, who got on.

Mr Potato Head, thinking Woody was trying to get rid of another toy, called to the others. "Get him! Toss him overboard!"

"No, no, wait!" But they pushed Woody into the street.

Woody bounced off the pavement and onto the car, right next to Buzz. "Thanks for the ride!" But the batteries ran out and the car slowed to a stop. Woody looked around. Seeing the sun through Buzz's helmet, he used it to focus sunlight on the rocket fuse. When the fuse lit, Woody grabbed Buzz and they rocketed towards the moving truck – but missed – and went soaring into the air!

Buzz popped open his wings, tearing away the rocket from his back. The two of them glided over Andy's van. "Hey, Buzz! You're flying!" They dipped through the sunroof and into an open box next to Andy. He let out a happy yell. "Hey! Wow! Woody! Buzz!"

A few months later, Woody, Buzz and the other toys were gathered around the baby monitor once again. It was their first Christmas in the new house and Andy was opening his presents.

Woody smiled. "Buzz Lightyear, you are not worried, are you?"

"Me? No, no. Are you?"

"Now, Buzz, what could Andy possibly get that is worse than you?"

Buzz glared at Woody, then the two toys smiled. They figured they were safe – at least until Andy's next birthday.

Do you think it's easy being a toy? Ask Woody and Buzz. They may not say anything to your face, but wait till you leave the room.